Disney's
Beauty and the Beast

Adapted by Teddy Slater
Illustrated by Ric Gonzalez and Ron Dias

A GOLDEN BOOK • NEW YORK
Western Publishing Company, Inc., Racine, Wisconsin 53404

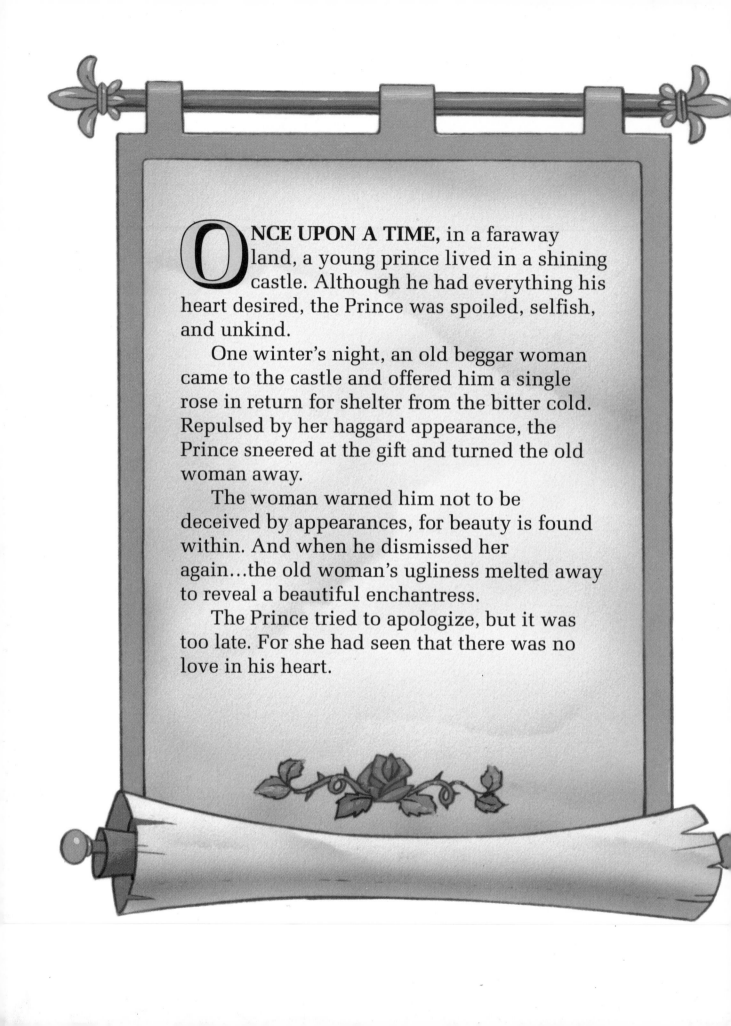

ONCE UPON A TIME, in a faraway land, a young prince lived in a shining castle. Although he had everything his heart desired, the Prince was spoiled, selfish, and unkind.

One winter's night, an old beggar woman came to the castle and offered him a single rose in return for shelter from the bitter cold. Repulsed by her haggard appearance, the Prince sneered at the gift and turned the old woman away.

The woman warned him not to be deceived by appearances, for beauty is found within. And when he dismissed her again...the old woman's ugliness melted away to reveal a beautiful enchantress.

The Prince tried to apologize, but it was too late. For she had seen that there was no love in his heart.

As punishment, the enchantress transformed the Prince into a hideous beast. Then she placed a powerful spell on the castle and all who lived there!

The rose she had offered was enchanted. It would bloom only until the Prince was twenty-one. If he could learn to love and be loved before the last petal fell, then the spell would be broken. If not, he would remain a beast for all time.

As the years passed, the Beast fell into despair. He did not believe that anyone could ever love him.

Slowly the rose began to wither.

In a nearby village there lived a young girl named Belle. She was very beautiful and a little bit odd. She cared only for her books and always felt out of place.

Her father, Maurice, was also a great reader. But while Belle read about adventure and romance, her father studied technical books. Maurice was an inventor—a genius, according to Belle; a crackpot, according to the townsfolk.

"Belle is even stranger than her father," the villagers whispered. "Her nose is always in a book, and her head is in the clouds."

Gaston, the most handsome man in town, wanted to make Belle his wife. But she always turned him down. She thought he was a slow-witted brute.

One cold day, Maurice hitched his horse, Philippe, to a wagon and set off to show his latest invention at a fair on the other side of the woods.

With his mind on the fair, Maurice got lost in the forest. An icy wind whistled through the trees, and he suddenly heard the howling of wolves. Spooked, Philippe bolted, and Maurice was thrown to the ground. To escape the wolves, the frightened man ran deeper and deeper into the woods.

At last Maurice came to a castle and stumbled inside. There he was greeted by Mrs. Potts the teapot, Cogsworth the mantelclock, and Lumiere the candelabra. But before he had time to marvel over these strange creatures, an even stranger one appeared—the Beast!

Maurice stared at the Beast in horror. The creature howled angrily, then scooped Maurice up and carried him off to a dungeon.

Meanwhile, Philippe had made his way back home. Belle saw the riderless horse and knew something had happened to her father.

"Philippe! Take me to him!" she cried, leaping astride the exhausted horse. Philippe gathered his strength and thundered off into the woods.

When Belle reached the castle, she searched
frantically for her father. The enchanted objects led her
to the tower, but just as she found Maurice, the Beast
appeared. Belle let out a terrified gasp.

When she realized that he was Maurice's captor,
Belle begged the Beast to free her father. She bravely
offered herself in Maurice's place, and the Beast
accepted. He led her to her room before Belle could
even bid her father good-bye.

"The castle is now your home," the Beast said
gruffly. Belle was free to go anywhere she liked—
except the West Wing.

That night Belle slipped out of her room and found
her way to the forbidden West Wing. She discovered
the Beast's foul lair, but he was nowhere in sight.

Belle was drawn to the enchanted rose she saw by
the window. But when she reached out to touch it, the
Beast suddenly appeared at the window.

Belle screamed and fled from the room.

Belle ran out of the castle, mounted Philippe, and escaped into the night. But a pack of wolves soon had the girl and her horse surrounded. Belle was helpless.

Suddenly the Beast appeared. A terrible snarling and howling arose as the Beast and the wolves battled for their lives. At last the wolves ran off, leaving the Beast badly injured.

Belle knew she couldn't leave him there, so she brought the Beast back to the castle and bound his wounds. Gentle as she was, the Beast roared in agony.

"I barely touched you," said Belle. Then she saw a look of pain on his face. "I forgot to thank you for saving my life," she added softly.

The Beast only grunted in reply. But her words touched him.

In the days that followed, the Beast tried to be a proper host. He showed Belle his library, where they read together, and she, in return, began to teach him how to act like a gentleman.

"Perhaps it isn't too late," Cogsworth whispered to Mrs. Potts and her son, Chip the teacup. "If Belle can only love the Beast, this dreadful spell may yet be broken."

The winter passed pleasantly for Belle and the Beast. Belle thought of him as her dearest friend. He dreamt of little but the beautiful Belle.

One night while Belle was showing him how to dance, the Beast stammered, "Belle, are you happy here—with me?"

"Yes," said Belle, but the Beast saw a trace of sadness in her eyes. Then Belle added, "If only I could see my father again, even for a minute."

"You can," the Beast said,
handing her a magic mirror.

Belle gazed into it with
wonder. She saw Maurice trudging
through the forest. He looked frail and old.
Even as she watched, her father collapsed in a heap.
    "I must go to him!" Belle cried. "He may be dying."
    "I release you," the Beast said sadly. "But take
the mirror. Then you will always have a way
to remember me."

With the magic mirror to guide her, Belle soon found her father and brought him back to their cottage. But their happy reunion was cut short by a pounding on the door.

"We've come to take Maurice to Maison des Loons," announced Monsieur D'Arque, director of the village's insane asylum.

"No!" Belle cried. "My father isn't crazy!"

Gaston's friend Lefou stepped forward. "Maurice has been raving that you were imprisoned by a hideous beast," he said. "Only a crazy man would tell such a tale."

"But it's true," Belle protested. She searched the angry crowd and saw Gaston. "Gaston!" she cried. "You know my father isn't crazy. Tell them."

Gaston told her that he might be able to calm the crowd—if Belle would promise to marry him.

"Never!" Belle exclaimed. "And my father is not crazy. There really is a Beast and I can prove it. Look in the mirror and see."

The crowd looked at the Beast's reflection and grew frightened.

Gaston was furious at Belle's refusal. "We must hunt down this savage animal!" he cried, stirring up the mob. "Who's with me?"

"We are!" answered the villagers. They locked Belle and her father in the cellar of their cottage and rode off to storm the Beast's castle.

Luckily Chip, Mrs. Potts's son, had stowed away in Belle's saddlebag. He used Maurice's latest invention to release Belle and her father from the cellar.

By the time Belle reached the castle, Gaston and the Beast were in a mortal duel on the castle roof. The Beast managed to knock Gaston's weapon from his hand, and there was nothing to stop him from killing Gaston—nothing but the Beast's own humanity.

Gaston screamed for mercy. The Beast granted it and turned away from his foe. At once, the ungrateful Gaston rose up and plunged a knife into the Beast's back.

The Beast roared in pain, frightening Gaston, who lost his footing and fell off the roof into the fog below.

Belle flew to the Beast's side.

"You came back," the Beast said weakly. "At least I got to see you one last time."

"No! No!" Belle said, sobbing, as she kissed him. "Please don't die.... I love you."

At that instant the spell was broken, and in a shower of enchanted rain, the Beast became a handsome prince. Even the enchanted servants returned to their human forms.

The castle came alive with rejoicing as the young Prince gathered Belle into his arms. Mrs. Potts, Cogsworth, and Lumiere had not one doubt that the loving couple would live happily ever after.